CONTENTS

- The birth of Ganesha

- Lord Ganesha's different forms and poses and their meaning

- Ganesh Chaturthy and its significance

- History of Ganesh Chaturthy

- Facts about Ganesha that nobody knows

- Ganesh Chaturthy celebrations around the world

- Why we worship Ganesha first

- How to do Ganesha pooja at home

- 108 names of Ganesha

The Divine story of Lord Ganesha

Although he is known by many attributes, Ganesha's elephant head makes him easy to identify. Ganesha is widely revered as the remover of obstacles, the patron of arts and sciences and the deva of intellect and wisdom. As the god of beginnings, he is honoured at the start of rites and ceremonies.

The birth of Ganesha:

One day Goddess Parvati was at home on Mount Kailash preparing for a bath. As she didn't want to be disturbed, she told Nandi, her husband Shiva's Bull, to guard the door and let no one pass. Nandi faithfully took his post, intending to carry out Parvati's wishes. But, when Shiva came home and naturally wanted to come inside, Nandi had to let him pass, being loyal first to Shiva. Parvati was angry at this slight, but even more than this, at the fact that she had no one as loyal to Herself as Nandi was to Shiva. So, taking the turmeric paste (for bathing) from her body and breathing life into it, she created Ganesha, declaring him to be her own loyal son.

The next time Parvati wished to bathe, she posted Ganesha on guard duty at the door. In due course, Shiva came home, only to find this strange boy telling him he couldn't enter his own house! Furious, Shiva ordered his army to destroy the boy, but they all failed! Such power did Ganesha possess, being the son of Devi Herself!

This surprised Shiva. Seeing that this was no ordinary boy, the usually peaceful Shiva decided he would have to fight him, and in his divine fury severed Ganesha's head, killing him instantly. When Parvati learned of this, she was so enraged and insulted that she decided to destroy the entire Creation! Lord Brahma, being the Creator, naturally had his issues with this, and pleaded that she reconsider her drastic plan. She said she would, but only if two conditions were met: one, that Ganesha be brought back to life, and two, that he be forever worshipped before all the other gods.

Shiva, having cooled down by this time, and realizing his mistake, agreed to Parvati's conditions. He sent Brahma out with orders to bring back the head of the first creature he crosses that is laying with its head facing North. Brahma soon returned with the head of a strong and powerful elephant, which Shiva placed onto Ganesha's body. Breathing new life into him, he declared Ganesha to be his own son as well, and gave him the status of being foremost among the gods, and leader of all the ganas (classes of beings), Ganapati.

Meaning of the story of Ganesh:

Parvati is a form of Devi, the Parashakti (Supreme Energy). In the human body She resides in the Muladhara chakra as the Kundalini shakti. It is said that when we purify ourselves, ridding ourselves of the impurities that bind us, then the Lord automatically comes. This is why Shiva, the Supreme Lord, came unannounced as Parvati was bathing.

Nandi, Shiva's bull, who Parvati first sent to guard the door represents the divine temperment. Nandi is so devoted to Shiva that his every thought is directed to Him, and he is able to easily recognize the Lord when He arrives. This shows that the attitude of the spiritual aspirant is what gains access to Devi's (the kundalini shakti's) abode. One must first develop this attitude of the devotee before hoping to become qualified for the highest treasure of spiritual attainment, which Devi alone grants.

After Nandi permitted Shiva to enter, Parvati took the turmeric paste from Her own body, and with it created Ganesha..

Yellow is the color associated with the Muladhara chakra, where the kundalini resides, and Ganesha is the deity who guards this chakra. Devi needed to create Ganesha, who represents the earthbound awareness, as a shield to protect the divine secret from unripe minds. It is when this awareness begins to turn away from things of the world, and toward the Divine, as Nandi had, that the great secret is revealed.

Shiva is the Lord and Supreme Teacher. Ganesha here represents the ego-bound Jiva. When the Lord comes, the Jiva, surrounded as it is with the murky cloud of ego, usually doesn't recognize Him, and maybe even ends up arguing or fighting with Him! Therefore, it is the duty of the Lord, in the form of the Guru, to cut off the head of our ego! So powerful is this ego however, that at first the Guru's instructions may not work, as Shiva's armies failed to subdue Ganesha. It often requires a tougher approach, but, eventually the compassionate Guru, in His wisdom finds a way.

Shiva restoring life to Ganesha, and replacing his head with an elephant's, means that before we can leave the body, the Lord first replaces our small ego with a "big", or universal ego. This doesn't mean that we become more egoistic. On the contrary, we no longer identify with the limited individual self, but rather with the large universal Self. In this way, our life is renewed, becoming one that can truly benefit Creation. It is however only a functional ego, like the one Krishna and Buddha kept. It is like a thin string tying the liberated Consciousness to our world, solely for our benefit.

Ganesha is given dominion over the Ganas, which is a general term denoting all classes of beings, ranging from insects, animals and humans to the subtle and celestial beings.

Such is the greatness of Sri Ganesha! Jai Ganesha!

Lord Ganesha Forms and Postures

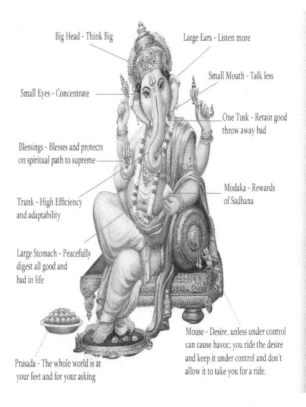

Big Head - Think Big

Large Ears - Listen more

Small Mouth - Talk less

Small Eyes - Concentrate

One Tusk - Retain good throw away bad

Blessings - Blesses and protects on spiritual path to supreme

Trunk - High Efficiency and adaptability

Modaka - Rewards of Sadhana

Large Stomach - Peacefully digest all good and bad in life

Mouse - Desire, unless under control can cause havoc; you ride the desire and keep it under control and don't allow it to take you for a ride.

Prasada - The whole world is at your feet and for your asking

There are almost 32 ganesha forms based on the characteristics:-

- Bala Ganesha
- Taruna Ganesha
- Bhakti Ganesha
- Vira Ganesha
- Shakthi Ganesha
- Dvija Ganesha
- Siddhi Ganesha
- Ucchista Ganesha
- Vighna Ganesha
- Kshipra Ganesha
- Heramba Ganesha
- Lakshmi Ganesha
- Maha Ganesha
- Vijaya Ganesha
- Nritya Ganesha
- Urdhva Ganesha
- Ekakshara Ganesha
- Varada Ganesha
- Tryakshara Ganesha
- Kshipra prasada Ganesha
- Haridra Ganesha
- Ekadanta Ganesha
- Shristi Ganesha
- Uddanda Ganesha

- Rinamochana Ganesha
- Dhuddhi Ganesha
- Dwimukha Ganesha
- Trimukha Ganesha
- Sinha Ganesha
- Yoga
- Durga Ganesha
- Sankatahara Ganesha

Ganesha is one of the most famous and greatly worshiped deities in Hinduism. The main identity of Ganesha is his elephant like head. Lord Ganesha is invoked as Vighneswara at the launch of an event or business by majority of the Hindus as he is believed to be the obstacle remover. Lord Ganesha is also considered as the God of auspicious beginnings and bestower of fortune in abundance. He is the son of Lord Shiva and Hindu Goddess Parvati. Ganesha is known by many names and has many different forms. The Ganesha Purana describes the 32 forms of Lord Ganesha and among them, Mahaganapathi is widely worshiped. The first 16 forms of Ganesha are known by the name "Shodasa Ganapati" and the later ones are known as "Ekavimsathi".

There are several layers of intricate meaning behind each part of Lord Ganesha.

Different Forms of Lord Ganesha:

He is represented in various forms across the Hindu society. Bala Ganapati is one of the most adored depictions of Ganesha with his childlike nature. He has sugarcane, mango and a jackfruit in his hands and his favorite modaka, a sweet in his trunk.

Vira Ganapati

As Vira Ganapati he is depicted as a brave heart. Resplendent with a range of weapons in his several hands. Some of the weapons he holds are bow, sword, gada, spear, shield, battle axe and many more. Ganesha 's form might not instill fear among most people because of his child like qualities but according to Hindu mythology ganesha is a force to be reckoned with both physically and also intellectually. He stops the mighty Shiva from seeing parvati on orders from his mother parvati, which made lord Shiva furious and slay his head. Similarly In a bid to win the fruit, he acts smartly and goes around his parents and outruns kartikeya who went around the world thrice. These acts are proof to the mighty strength and intellect of vigneshwarar.

Vighna Ganapati

Vighna Ganapati, "Lord of Obstacles," is of brilliant gold hue and bedecked in jewels. His eight arms hold a noose and goad, tusk and modaka, conch and discus, a bouquet of flowers, sugar cane, flower arrow and an axe.

Handsome, red-hued Kshipra Ganapati,"Quick-acting" giver of boons, displays His broken tusk, a noose, goad and a sprig of the kalpavriksha (wish-fulfilling) tree. In His uplifted trunk He holds a tiny pot of precious jewels.

Lakshmi Ganapathi

In the form of Lakshmi Ganapati he stands flanked by lakshmi the goddess of wealth. He holds the varada mudra in his hand

and a sprig of kalpavriksha. Worshipping Lakshmi Ganapati is said to bless the devotee with wealth wisdom and knowledge.

Nritya Ganapati

Ganapati is also depicted in his dancing form as Nritya Ganapati. Where he is depicted as dancing under the kalpa vriksha with great eccentricity and exuberance. In most depictions he is shown raising his right leg and the left leg is placed on the earth. This signifies the élan and grace with which he moves. It is believed that Ganesha used to entertain his parents and other gods with his dance.

In almost all depictions Ganesha is shown with his vahana the mouse. This symbolizes how a small mouse with the blessings of Ganesha can serve as the vahana for the lord himself. Some other meaning also say that the mouse signifies ego, arrogance and evil traits in us. Lord Ganesha sitting on the mouse means that one has to control all his desires and negative traits to attain blessings from god.

In the standing posture he remains straight with no bend in his posture. It is called as abhanga. This is a very formal depiction of lord Ganesha. Even in his standing posture he is shown as having one leg on the ground and another on his vahana, the mouse.

Another important posture of Ganesha that is commonly seen is the sitting posture. He is mostly seated on a lotus or a simhasana (throne). The pose is called as lalitasana in which one leg is folded and other is placed freely on the ground. The leg that touches the ground denotes that Ganesha is concerned about the worldly affairs to help his devotees. In another variation of the sitting pose he is seen sitting cross legged. This is a meditative pose.

In many paintings and artistic sculptures he is seen as reclined on a bed like structure. This gives the idol a royal and luxurious look. Such statues are said to bring the worshiper wealth, prosperity, comfort, success and luxury.

As the Sankatahara Ganapati, He is the dispeller of sorrow. He is seated on a lotus and has four arms holding a bowl of pudding, a goad and a noose while gesturing the boon-granting varada mudra. He also has His consort with Him.

Durga Ganapati

As Durga Ganapati, He is the invincible Ganapati paying tribute to Mother Durga and is depicted with 8 arms holding a bow and arrow, goad and noose, prayer beads, a rose apple and his broken tusk.

There also forms of Ganapati with two and three faces,they are called as dwimukha ganapati and trimukha ganapati respectively.

Placing a ganesha idol or picture in the home is one of the first and foremost activities of any homeowner. This is because the statues of ganesha remove obstacles, bring luck and ensure success to the devotee. But one has to be careful while choosing idols for the home. It is preferable that one chooses a vinayaka idol with the trunk curved towards the left. When the trunk curves right, it is called valampuri vinayaka. The sun`s energies flow through the trunk. This form of Ganesha is called Siddhi Vinayaka, as it can immediately yield desired results. It needs special worship and one has to be very careful in keeping such idols at home. If prayers are not done as per Vedic rules, then it incurs the anger of the residing Lord and as the heat principle is governed by the Lord Sun, it burns away good results. Rules should never be violated and pooja should be done at the right time, in the right suitable way, which is very difficult for householders to adhere to. The dakshinabhimukhi idol or idol of Ganesha with trunk curved right is not usually worshipped at home as there is an emission of frequency waves coming from the south called Tiryak or raja frequency. When all Vedic norms are followed meticulously and worshipped accordingly, then it increases the sattwa or highly positive vibrations that can withstand the raja frequencies emitted from the south direction. When idols with trunk curved right are worshipped, it bestows boons of moksha or salvation. It liberates the soul from worldly fetters.

Idols with Straight Trunk are also made, these kinds of idols are hard to find, but are considered special. The idol with the trunk of Lord Ganesha in the air represents a state where his 'Kundalini' reached the peak. These idols are always good for any home and office.

For those who are fond of the artistic forms of ganesha that are available in the market, there is a word of caution. It is said that those idols do not conform to our traditional scriptures that describe how a ganesha idol should be. Artistic idols can be creatively used in interior decoration to bring in positive energy but they should not be worshipped or placed inside the puja room. Also when buying idols for pooja it is advisable to avoid dancing forms or nritya ganeshas and also statues that exceed the height of 18 inches.

Ganesha is the remover of obstacles that is why he is fondly called as vigneshwara. Worship towards ganesha can bring the person success in all his endeavors and also bless him with great intellect and wisdom.

What is Ganesh Chaturthi? Why is it celebrated?

Ganesh Chaturthi is a ten-day Hindu festival celebrated to honour the elephant-headed God Ganesha's birthday. He is the younger son of Lord Shiva and Goddess Parvati.

Ganesha is known by 108 different names and is the Lord of arts and sciences and the deva of wisdom. He is honoured at the start of rituals and ceremonies as he's considered the God of beginnings. He's widely and dearly referred to as Ganapati or Vinayaka.

There are two different versions about Ganesha's birth. One has it that Goddess

Parvati created Ganesha out of dirt off her body while having a bath and set him to guard her door while she finishes her bath. Shiva who has gone out, returned at that time, but as Ganesha didn't know of him, stopped him from entering. An angry Shiva severed the head of Ganesha after a combat between the two. Parvati was enraged and Shiva promised Ganesha will live again. The devas who went in search of a head facing north of a dead person could manage only the head of an elephant. Shiva fixed the elephant's head on the child and brought him back to life.

The other legend has it that Ganesha was created by Shiva and Parvati on request of the Devas, to be a vighnakartaa (obstacle-creator) in the path of rakshasas (demonic beings), and a vighnahartaa (obstacle-averter) to help the Devas.

The festival begins on Shukla Chaturthi which is the fourth day of the waxing moon period, and ends on the 14th day of the waxing moon period known as Anant Chaturdashi.

Maharashtra is the state known for grand scale Ganesh Chaturthi celebrations.

During the festival, colourful pandals (temporary shrines) are setup and the Lord is worshiped for ten days.

There are four main rituals during the festival - Pranapratishhtha - the process of infusing the deity into a murti or idol, Shhodashopachara - 16 forms of paying tribute to Ganesha, Uttarpuja - Puja after which the idol could be shifted after it's infusion, Ganpati Visarjan - immersion of the Idol in the river.

Foodies wait for Modak, a sweet dish prepared using rice or flour stuffed with grated jaggery, coconuts and dry fruits. The plate containing the Modak is supposed to be filled with twenty-one pieces of the sweet.

The festival was celebrated as a public event since the time of Maratha King Shivaji, but a Sarvajanik (Public) Ganesh idol was installed first by Bhausaheb Laxman Javale.

Lokmanya Tilak changed the festival from a private celebration to a grand public event "to bridge the gap between Brahmins and non-Brahmins and find an appropriate context in which to build a new grassroots unity between them"

Lord Ganesha is also worshiped in Thailand, Cambodia, Indonesia, Afghanistan, Nepal and China.

The Story Behind Ganesh Chaturthi

Ganesh Chaturthi is one of the major festivals celebrated in India with great enthusiasm and devotion. The festival marks the birthday of Lord Ganesha; the Lord of knowledge, wisdom, prosperity and good fortune. The festival is also known as Vinayak Chaturthi or Vinayak Chavithi. This day, observed as one of the most auspicious in the Hindu religion, is widely celebrated especially in the state of Maharashtra.

How Ganesh chaturthy is being started?

The exact date of starting of puja on the Ganesha Chaturthi festival is not known by anyone however, according to the history it has been estimated that Ganesh Chaturthi was getting celebrated as a public event in the Pune during the time of Shivaji (founder of the Maratha Empire) during 1630 to 1680. Since Shivaji's time, it was started celebrating regularly as Ganesha was Kuladevata of their empire. After end of Peshwas, it remained as a family celebration however revived again in 1893 by the Lokmanya Tilak (an Indian freedom fighter and social reformer).

Ganesha Chaturthi was started celebrating by the Hindu people as an annual domestic festival with a huge preparation. Gradually, it was started celebrating as a national festival to remove the conflicts between Brahmins and non-Brahmins as well as bring unity among people. People in the Maharashtra started celebrating this festival with lots of courage and nationalistic fervour during the British rule in order to get free from the cruel behaviour of Britishers. The ritual of Ganesh Visarjan was established by the Lokmanya Tilak.

Gradually, this festival was started celebrating by the people through community participation instead of family celebration.

People of the society and community, get together to celebrate this festival as a community festival and to perform intellectual speech, recite poetry, dance, devotional songs, play, musical concerts, folk dances, recite mantras, aarti and many more activities in the group. People meet together before date and decide everything about celebration as well as how to control over large crowd.

Ganesh Chaturthi, a sacred Hindu festival, is celebrated by the people as a birth day of the Lord Ganesha (a God of God, means supreme God of wisdom and prosperity). The whole Hindu community celebrates together annually with full devotion and dedication. According to the Hindu mythology, it is believed that Ganesh was born on Chaturthi (4th day of bright fortnight) in Magh month. Since then, birth date of Lord Ganesha was started celebrating as Ganesh Chaturthi. Now-a-days, it is celebrated all over the world by the people of Hindu community.

Celebration

Ganesh Chaturthi preparations commence from almost a month before the festival. The celebrations last for around ten days (from Bhadrapad Shudh Chaturthi to Ananta Chaturdashi). On the first day a clay idol of Lord Ganesha is installed in homes. Homes are decorated with flowers. Temples witness the visit of large number of devotees. Poojas are performed and bhajans are chanted. Often, families gather together to celebrate the festival. Localities organize and arrange for pandals and install large idols of Lord Ganesha to celebrate the festival with friends and family. On the final day of the celebrations, the idol of Lord Ganesha is taken on the streets. People exhibit their enthusiasm and joy in the form of dancing and singing on the streets along with the idol. The idol is finally immersed in the river or sea. The day witnesses a large number of devotees expressing their happiness and offering their prayers.

Some facts about Lord Ganesha no one knows

* The son of Shiva and Parvati, Ganesha has an elephantine countenance with a curved trunk and big ears, and a huge pot-bellied body of a human being. He is the Lord of success and destroyer of evils and obstacles. He is also worshipped as the god of education, knowledge, wisdom and wealth. In fact, Ganesha is one of the five prime Hindu deities (Brahma, Vishnu, Shiva and Durga being the other four) whose idolatry is glorified as the panchayatana puja.

* According to Shivpuran, it was Parvati's friends Jaya and Vijaya's decision to make Lord Ganesha. They had suggested Parvati that Nandi and other follow the instructions of Lord Shiva only. Therefore, there should be someone who follows Parvati's orders too.

Hence, Parvati made Ganesha from the dirt of her body.

- According to Shiva Maha Puran, the body colour of Lord Ganesha is green and red.

- According to Brahmavavart Puran, Goddess Parvati had kept Punyak fast for a baby boy. As a result of this fast only, Lord Krishna in disguise of a baby boy came to Parvati.
- According to Brahmavavart Puran, when all the Gods were blessing Lord Ganesha, Shani Dev was standing with his head facing downwards. When Parvati asked the reason for this act, he replied that if he looks directly at Ganesha, he will lose his head. But Parvati insisted and Shani Dev looked at

Ganesha. This resulted in Ganesha losing his head from his body.

- According to Brahmavavart Puran, when Ganesha's head got separated from his body when Shani Dev looked at him directly, that time lord Shrihari flew on his Garud towards north direction and reached River side of Pushpbhadra. There a female elephant was sleeping with her newly born baby elephant. He cut the baby elephant's head and put it on Ganesha's body and brought him back to life.

- According to Brahmavavart Puran, Lord Shiva in anger had once attacked Surya Dev with his Trishul. Surya Dev's father got annoyed with Shiva and cursed him that thw way he has harmed his son's body, one day his son's will be cut from his body.

- According to Brahmavavart Puran, one day Tulsidevi was crossing through the banks of Ganges. That time Ganesha was meditating there. Seeing Ganesha, Tulsidevi got attracted towards him. She asked him to marry her, but Ganesha refused to do so. In anger, Tulsi cursed Ganesha that he will marry soon and Ganesha in return cursed her to be a plant.

* According to Shiva Maha Puran, Ganesha's marriage was fixed with Riddhi and Siddhi. He had two sons – Shetra and Laabh.
* According to Shiva Maha Puran, when Lord Shiva was going to destroy Tripur, an akashvani happened that till the time he worships Ganesha, he won't be able to destroy Tripur. Then Shiva called Bhadrakali and did Gajanan Puja. He won the battle.
* According to Brahmavavart Puran, when Parshuram went to Kailash Mountain to meet Shiva, he was

meditating. Lord Ganesha did not allow Parshuram to meet Shiva. Parshuram got angry and attacked Ganesha. The weapon he used to attack Ganesha was given to him by Lord Shiva only. Ganesha did not want the attack to go waste as it was his father's weapon, so he took the attack in his teeth and thus lost one of his teeth. Since then he is known as Ekdant.

- Mahabharat epic has been written by Lord Ganesha.

- According to Ganesh Puran, there are 8 Gana in Chandpuran – Magan, Nagan, yagan, jagan, bhagan, ragan, sagan and tagan. Alphabets are also known as Gana.
- According to Ganesh Puran, the muladhar chakra of a human body is also known as Ganesha.

Muladhara-Chakra
(Root chakra)

Ganesh Chaturthi celebrations around the world

Ganesh Chaturthi, one of the most popular festivals in India brings people from all caste, religion and creed together. The 10-days festival is celebrated usually in August or September depending on the Hindu calendar.

The legends say that Ganesh Chaturthi was being celebrated as a public event in Pune since the times of Shivaji (1630-1680), the founder of the Maratha Empire. However, in 1893, Lokmanya Tilak transformed the annual domestic festival into a large, well-organised event to bring people together.

Though this festival is celebrated across India, the states like Maharashtra, Tamil Nadu, Kerala and Goa are the top states for celebrating this festival with big enthusiasm. With Indians residing in every corner of the world, this festival is more like international now. So, we take you to the countries, apart from India, where you can enjoy this festival of love, happiness, celebrations, colours and festive dishes. Countries like Canada, Mauritius, Thailand, Singapore, Cambodia, Burma, US, UK and Fiji celebrate this festival and many of mentioned countries' government have declared a public holiday for that day.

Ganeshotsav is been celebrated in Mauritius since 1982 by local Hindu community which consists of 52 % of the total population on this island. In fact the first day of this festival is a public holiday in Mauritius. Though not on a large scale, the festival is celebrated in the regional temples or individual homes. It is glorious to celebrate this festival in the temple as the Ganesh idols made out of mud are established at temples and homes. Devotees visit temples, offer aarti and perform a traditional dance.

Canada

Toronto, the capital of Canada has many Indians that get the Ganesh idol from their respective home in India. Even with limited resources they make it grand by coming together, sing aarti and share the prasad. They still continue to follow the typical Indian culture during this festival.

USA

With a large Indian community residing in the US, the festival is celebrated on a large scale. They import idols from Mumbai and the celebrations continue till the 11th day. The festival attracts over 10,000 visitors in the states. The big puja features aarti, music and dance in the cultural environment.

United Kingdom

Hounslow, the principle town in London also welcomes Lord Ganesha on a large scale.

More than 5000 people show up every year for the celebration of this festival. The idol is placed at the Laxmi Narayan Temple followed by a grand aarti, with traditional food, dance and fancy dress competition throughout the days. It ends with a procession to Ham, where the idol is immersed in the Thames followed by 4000 devotees, police protection and 50 volunteers ensure people's safety.

Ganesh Chaturthi is best celebrated with the spirit of enthusiasm for the supreme

God of wisdom, fortune, prosperity and remover of all obstacles. No matter where you are the spirit of devotion for Lord Ganesha is intact with every Indian.

Reasons Why We Worship Ganesha First

Lord Ganesha is a popular deity of Hinduism. He is denoted by His elephant head, big belly, His mount and a small mouse. Ganesha epitomises wisdom and knowledge. He is the Vighnaharta or the destroyer of all obstacles. Ganesha's elephant head is the symbol of wisdom, and His long ears signify that He hears everything that His devotees say. In India, Lord Ganesha is worshiped before the commencement of almost every task. He is worshiped first in almost all rituals of Hinduism. In fact, Lord Ganesha is almost synonymous with the beginning of any work. Ever wondered why is it that we worship Ganesha first? Let's find out. What The Scriptures Say According to the Ganapati Upanishad, Lord Ganesha appeared even before the creation of nature (prakriti) and consciousness (purusha). This is an important link as to why Lord Ganesha is worshiped before beginning any task. According to this scriptures, Lord Ganesha is eternal and He appeared even before the process of creation. Mythology Once Goddess Parvati instructed Lord Ganesha to guard the gates and not to let anybody enter. As Ganesha stood on guard, Lord Shiva came and headed towards his room. When He was prevented from entering the house by Ganesha, Lord Shiva became furious and chopped off Ganesha's head. Hearing Ganesha's scream, Goddess Parvati came running and on seeing Ganesha's plight she became furious. She pledged to destroy the world if Her son was not brought back to life. Then Lord Shiva replaced Ganesha's head with an elephant's and brought Him back to life. Seeing this condition of Her son, Parvati became extremely sad. So, Lord Shiva bestowed Ganesha with divine powers and declared that no puja or good work will ever be deemed complete without invoking Lord Ganesha's name and blessings. Hence, Lord Ganesha became the 'pratham pujya' or the one who is worshiped first. Another myth about Ganesha being worshipped first goes like this. Once Ganesha's elder brother Kartikeya declared that He was the best among all Gods. So, Lord Shiva suggested that He and Ganesha would contest a race by circling the universe. The one who returns first will be declared the winner and will be worshiped first. So, Kartikeya happily set out on His peacock to circle the universe. Lord Ganesha being the intelligent one, circled around His parents because for Him his parents were the Universe. So, Ganesha was declared the winner and hence Lord Ganesha is worshiped first. Yogic Belief According to the yogic perspective, anything we do has to fall under one of the two categories: material or spiritual. It is believed that Lord Ganesha rules the 'muladhara chakra' of our body. 'Muladhara' is the interface between the material and the spiritual worlds. Lord Ganesha is said to control both these worlds. He is the one who gives the material enjoyments in this world and He is the one who liberates us from the endless cycle of birth and death. According to the yogic principles, our material life as well as our spiritual journey starts from the 'Muladhara' chakra which is controlled by Lord Ganesha. Hence, to complete our life cycle without any obstacles, we need the blessings of Lord Ganesha. Since He is the one who gets rid of all the obstacles from our lives, we worship Lord Ganesha before beginning any important work.

How to do Ganesha Puja at home?

However, praying to Ganesha throughout the year has a host of benefits that include the following:

- It improves earnings
- Makes you financially sound
- Improves education
- Helps you grow in career

* Helps get over all obstacles in life

Worshipping Ganesha does not require a lot of effort and you should preferably do it on a Wednesday. If you can, do observe a fast on that day as well. Also, for Prasad, prepare some laddoos or modak, as this is one of the favourite foods of Ganesha.

For the main puja, do the following:

Place a idol of Ganesha on a piece of orange cloth --- However, instead of a using Ganesha in a sitting posture, use one in which he is standing.

This will reap better benefits for you. You should also light a lamp in front of his picture after that.

After that, offer Jasmin, marigold or other flowers during praying.

While praying recite the mantra, Om Ganeshaya Namah.

After that, can also read the Ganesha Chalisa and do his aarti.

Post that, offer some modak and laddoo to the Lord and close your eyes. You can later distribute the same as Prasad.

During Ganesh Chaturthi, the procedure for Ganesha Puja is slightly different and elaborate. However, no matter how you pray to Ganesha, it will always reap great dividends for you.

108 Names of Lord Ganesha

1. Akhuratha

One who has Mouse as His Charioteer

2. Alampata

Ever Eternal Lord

3. Ami

Incomparable Lord

4. Anantachidrupamayam

Infinite and Consciousness Personified

5. Avaniish

Lord of the whole World

6. Avighna

Remover of Obstacles

7.Balaganapati

Beloved and Lovable Child

8. Bhalchandra

Moon-Crested Lord

9. Bheema

Huge and Gigantic

10. Bhupati

Lord of the Gods

11. Bhuvanpati

God of the Gods

12. Buddhinat

God of Wisdom

13. Buddhipriya

Knowledge Bestower

14. Buddhividhata

God of Knowledge

15. Chaturbhuj

One who has Four Arms

16. Devadeva

Lord of All Lords

17. Devantakanashakarin

Destroyer of Evils and Asuras

18. Devavrata

One who accepts all Penances

19. Devendrashika

Protector of All Gods

20. Dharmik

One who gives Charity

21. Dhoomravarna

Smoke-Hued Lord

22. Durja

Invincible Lord

23. Dvaimatura

One who has two Mothers

24. Ekaakshara

He of the Single Syllable

25. Ekadanta

Single-Tusked Lord

26. Ekadrishta

Single-Tusked Lord

27. Eshanputra

Lord Shiva's Son

28. Gadadhara

One who has The Mace as His Weapon

29. Gajakarna

One who has Eyes like an Elephant

30. Gajanana

Elephant-Faced Lord

31. Gajananeti

Elephant-Faced Lord

32. Gajavakra

Trunk of The Elephant

33. Gajavaktra

One who has Mouth like an Elephant

34. Ganadhakshya

Lord of All Ganas (Gods)

35. Ganadhyakshina

Leader of All The Celestial Bodies

36. Ganapati

Lord of All Ganas (Gods)

37. Gaurisuta

The Son of Gauri (Parvati)

38. Gunina

One who is The Master of All Virtues

39. Haridra

One who is Golden Coloured

40. Heramba

Mother's Beloved Son

41. Kapila

Yellowish-Brown Coloured

42. Kaveesha

Master of Poets

43. Kirti

Lord of Music

44. Kripalu

Merciful Lord

45. Krishapingaksha

Yellowish-Brown Eyed

46. Kshamakaram

The Place of Forgiveness

47. Kshipra

One who is easy to Appease

48. Lambakarna

Large-Eared Lord

49. Lambodara

The Huge Bellied Lord

50. Mahabala

Enormously Strong Lord

51. Mahaganapati

Omnipotent and Supreme Lord

52. Maheshwaram

Lord of The Universe

53. Mangalamurti

All Auspicious Lord

54. Manomay

Winner of Hearts

55. Mrityuanjaya

Conqueror of Death

56. Mundakarama

Abode of Happiness

57. Muktidaya

Bestower of Eternal Bliss

58. Musikvahana

One who has Mouse as His Charioteer

59. Nadapratithishta

One who Appreciates and Loves Music

60. Namasthetu

Vanquisher of All Evils and Vices and Sins

61. Nandana

Lord Shiva's Son

62. Nideeshwaram

Giver of Wealth and Treasures

63. Omkara

One who has the Form Of OM

64. Pitambara

One who has Yellow-Coloured Body

65. Pramoda

Lord of All Abodes

66. Prathameshwara

First Among All

67. Purush

The Omnipotent Personality

68. Rakta

One who has Red-Coloured Body

69. Rudrapriya

Beloved Of Lord Shiva

70. Sarvadevatman

Acceptor of All Celestial Offerings

71. Sarvasiddhanta

Bestower of Skills and Wisdom

72. Sarvatman

Protector of The Universe

73. Shambhavi

The Son of Parvati

74. Shashivarnam

One who has a Moon like Complexion

75. Shoorpakarna

Large-Eared Lord

76. Shuban

All Auspicious Lord

77. Shubhagunakanan

One who is The Master of All Virtues

78. Shweta

One who is as Pure as the White Colour

79. Siddhidhata

Bestower of Success and Accomplishments

80. Siddhipriya

Bestower of Wishes and Boons

81. Siddhivinayaka

Bestower of Success

82. Skandapurvaja

Elder Brother of Skand (Lord Kartik)

83. Sumukha

Auspicious Face

84. Sureshwaram

Lord of All Lords

85. Swaroop

Lover of Beauty

86. Tarun

Ageless

87. Uddanda

Nemesis of Evils and Vices

88. Umaputra

The Son of Goddess Uma (Parvati)

89. Vakratunda

Curved Trunk Lord

90. Varaganapati

Bestower of Boons

91. Varaprada

Granter of Wishes and Boons

92. Varadavinayaka

Bestower of Success

93. Veeraganapati

Heroic Lord

94. Vidyavaridhi

God of Wisdom

95. Vighnahara

Remover of Obstacles

96. Vignaharta

Demolisher of Obstacles

97. Vighnaraja

Lord of All Hindrances

98. Vighnarajendra

Lord of All Obstacles

99. Vighnavinashanaya

Destroyer of All Obstacles and Impediments

100. Vigneshwara

Lord of All Obstacles

101. Vikat

Huge and Gigantic

102. Vinayaka

Lord of All

103. Vishwamukha

Master of The Universe

104. Vishwaraja

King of The World

105. Yagnakaya

Acceptor of All Sacred and Sacrficial Offerings

106. Yashaskaram

Bestower of Fame and Fortune

107. Yashvasin

Beloved and Ever Popular Lord

108. Yogadhipa

The Lord of Meditation

Made in United States
Orlando, FL
29 April 2022

17319098R10043